Silent Voices

Tsapelo Thabeng

Pharos Books

ISBN: 978-93-55460-14-1
eISBN: 978-93-55460-17-2

Publisher: Pharos Books (P) Ltd.
Plot No.-55, Main Mother Dairy Road
Pandav Nagar, East Delhi-110092
Phone: +14049995474
WhatsApp: +14049995474
E-mail: sales@pharosbooks.in
Website: www.pharosbooks.in
Edition: 2022

Printed By: Sushma Book Binding House, Okhla Industrial Area, Phase II, New Delhi-110020

Silent Voices
Tsapelo Thabeng

Contents

About The Book

This is a compilation of poems and short stories written by Tsapelo Thabeng titled “Silent Voices”. It is her third book which released in 2021 in June after two books which she had been involved in namely “Lyrical Worsmiths” an anthology with other authors and her novel titled “From The Ashes”.

She has portrayed good artistic writing skills in poetry, short stories and writing novels. As she has been interviewed by the Midweek Sun about her book by Lame Chaba and appeared on Gabz FM as the poet she is.

My Word Speaks Volumes

Throw me a pen and a paper,
And let me narrate my story
No it's not a fairytale.
This is my heart poured out,
For your eyes to feast,
and your hearts to engulf.
Let my spirit lead you by the hand
Into the depth of my soul and mind.

Give me a pen and paper.
So that I write the first word,
The first letter.
That begins a journey to a
Destination unknown,
Let the ballpoint hit the paper
As the ink sticks.
As I let my hand speak what my mind
and heart agree on.
Pass me a pen and a paper.

So that I may give you
A glimpse of what I've been through,
As I show you my luna side,
And allow you to take a dive into
my reality versus my fantasy.
Please, continue to stick with me
As I drag you to my shadowed side
Where the stars, the moon, even the sun have faded
Where my dreamland turns into a land of the lost

On second thoughts
Don't give me a pen a paper now
But lend me your ears
And open your heart to my voice and words
Take the pen and paper and
let the world know who you really are
Don't let the ink run out or the paper crumble,
That's why I say…
Lend me your ears and open up your heart
'cause an artist never runs out of words
Nor does their journey end
Even when they are ash or dust!

Stolen Moments

If heaven had a post office I
would send you flowers
But instead I'm asking Angel Gabriel
To deliver a message to you
I'll knock on heaven's door If I have to,
Just to say....I miss and I love you
We both never got the chance,
To see each other grow.

My eyes are always filled with tears,
My heart is with pain,
Because I feel like you left too soon.
I never even said goodbye.
If I could turn back time
I would go back to the day,
I made you a mum.

And If I had one wish....one prayer
I would ask God,
To continue to make you my guardian angel
Thank you for loving me, mum!

Moulded Spear

Instruction…
It's not that I don't want to cry,
I have run out of tears.
My waterworks are dry
Like the Sahara Desert.
Each day my heart bled
Each time I felt a spear driven through my heart.

Construction…
It's not that I don't want to scream,
I became deaf to my own voice.
Ignored by my mind.
Deserted by own soul.
Let all the noise fade away
As my ears bled
So I kept silent.

Deliberation…
It's not that I don't want to fight.

I took flight on the wings
Of an angel, sent for me
By my King.
He showed me who I am to be.

Condemnation and destruction…
It's not that I am scared no, no, no
I have lost my energy to fear,
But, He became the light…

Introduction…
It is not that I am broken
I am simply a mould
Being shaped and sharpened like an arrow.

Of Royal Blood

They told me that
Prayer is one of the nutrients
Needed by a growing
Body, Mind & Soul
And they didn't forget
To let me know that
Faith is the ultimate,
Life changing aspect
'cause without it
Life is just a blowing wind,
With no direction.

Because of…
The depth of His love
The foundation He layed before me
By His stripes I'm healed
By His wounds I'm freed!

I may not show gratitude
Nor do I follow His footsteps 100%
But…
He continues to love me.
He continues to protect His lil' princess Yes! I'm royalty
I wear my crown with so much pride
As He is my Father
The King of all kings.

But how… God the Father made me
God the Son died for me, and…
God the Spirit lives in me
I will listen to you oh Father as You
Open my spiritual eyes,
Open my spiritual mind, but mostly
Open my spirutual heart
So that I may see You in Your own accordance,
So that I may be appeased in Your presence
Because in Your presence is where
I yearn to be…
Where my heart belongs!!!

Pride And Possession

The world is not cruel,
No the world is not unfair!
We are just afraid.
Soul and heart are just lost.
The mind is not at ease.
Who are we if we try to copy
Another's lifestyle.

We live everyday,
To fight another day.
WE! lose our true selves
Trying to please lost souls.
Stolen moments,
Heavy anchors.
Life paused
With no delay

We are alone in this race
It's not a relay.

Grab hold ahead,
And never let go.
Head held high
Chest out!
Smile so wide!
And teeth as white as the cloud!

Did I mention?
Your life is yours!
Pressure,
Is just a wrong turns.
Pleasure,
Is just endurance.

Take pride in who you are.
Possess every dream you have to!
Smile!
Everyday is a gift.
No wonder they
Say it's the present!

Short Stories

Convicted

It was a joyous day for the Mogale and Mompharing families, as their children were being united and the two families were becoming one. Abigail, being the youngest daughter to Mrs Mogale, who lost her husband two years ago, was finally tying the knot. All her three siblings were already in matrimonials and to her eyes, successful ones.

As Mrs Mogale prepared her daughter after Abigail's aunts left the room, she sat down and faced her daughter. She took her hands into hers and smiled with tears flooding her eyes. Abigail smiled at her mother with her dimples deepening and squeezing her mother's hands. "Don't start that mum, you know when you start to cry I start to cry as well – please don't." Her mother forced a smile, "It's just that I'm happy for you baby girl, today I'm becoming a mother-in-law – again." Abigail forced a quick fake smile. "I'm just happy that you grew out of that childish phase, that's all." Mrs Mogale cupped her daughter's face being careful not to mess up her make up.

All of a sudden her mind travelled back in time. When she first fell in love. The day that she knew her life, made sense and she had control. When she was young and found it odd not having any feelings towards any guy and the first guy, she went out with she was in tertiary school and her sister was encouraging her to try to "live a little" and let her hair down.

She went out with the guy for a couple of weeks and in those weeks, she felt nothing for him. Even when they kissed all that she got, was sick to her stomach. On her twentieth birthday, she went to a club with her sister and sisters-in-law just to celebrate. She bumped onto this tomboy who she got along with right off the bat. They started talking right there at the club and she invited her to hang with her siblings. There was something about her that intrigued her. She enjoyed her company and loved how free she was with her. They spent a lot of time together afterwards.

"I have to admit, I feel free when I'm with you, like I can be myself around you," Abigail said as she sat down next to Lesego. She put her hand on her thigh. For some reason, Abigail felt a rush in her body. She blushed and gave out a smile. "And I enjoy spending every minute with you, baby doll." Abigail cleared her throat and stared at her hands that played with each other. Lesego lifted her face with her thumb and got closer. Abigail looked at her for a few seconds and she kissed her, as her hand found its way to her face. Something deep inside her lit up. She has never felt such a rush in her body. She felt safe in both her arms and presence.

Things between Abigail and Lesego continued to reach the climax of joy in their lives. Lesego's family had already accepted her for who she was. Abigail wasn't even sure what to think of what was happening to her. She was "new" in this phase and she didn't even know what the phase was. "So how long has this been going on?" Abigail's sister said as she walked in on the two "love birds" who were cosy with each other in the living room watching television. Abigail cleared her throat and, "Hello to you too sister, please do come in and make yourself at home." She said as her sister sat down and took her glass of drink and finished it in one gulp. "Refreshing." She then winked at them. Abigail just scoffed.

"You guys look cute." "There is nothing going on between us B." Boingotlo stared at her little sister. "Girl please, you guys have been hanging out since you bumped into each other at the club and you, my dear sister, started glowing like nobody's business…and I think I might need some shades to look at you." Abigail chuckled. "You know mum will never approve of this…" Lesego cleared her throat and fixed herself on the sofa. "I know Abi-girl…she is too religious to approve such things but you know you have to tell her right? and the sooner you do it….the sooner she stops hooking you up." "And I choose later." "Huh?!" Lesego interrupted them. "Lesh…." "So you want to deceive your mother for how long?" "You don't know my mother Lesego…if she finds out that I'm…." "Lesbian…you can't even say it…..are you ashamed of who you are Abby?" "I'm not…it's just that….B do you mind..." Abigail's sister stood up and "I'm sorry I didn't mean to cause any problems between you too I just came to let you know that Ogopotse's uncles are coming over tomorrow and mum wanted me to ask you if you could come over and help out." "I'll call you a little later." "Ok sis….bye Lesh and again I love the two of you together." Abigail's sister then left.

"Lesh I don't even know what's going on with me ok….I don't know maybe it's just…" "A phase?" Lesego sounded angry. Her voice trembling with anger and disappointment. "Wake up Abigail…homosexuality isn't a "flu" that you can cure with a sleep and couple of tablets ok. It's not something you wake up and suddenly it's gone alright? We don't choose this. Do you know how many times I have to act all tough because God doesn't "approve" this. I've been bullied because of who I am. I was raped when I was 18 by guys because they said that I needed to taste the real thing, so that I snap out of my madness and for years I fought with my family about this. My own father cut me out of his life. My own mother had to choose between me and my father. I've been through enough heartache Abigail. I love you and I know this sounds cheesy but you the best thing that has ever happened to me…but if you don't know where you stand in your life…then I guess….this is goodbye."

"Lesh please wait." Abigail grabbed onto her arm. "I'm done waiting A….I'm done waiting for society to change its view on homosexuality. I'm done waiting for life to be fair for us and I'm gonna carry on with my life because at the end of it all I've got me to depend on right." She then left. Abigail felt like she was having a heart attack. She couldn't understand what was going on with her. Did she really develop feelings for Lesego and to top it all, could she be a lesbian?

Thoughts kept clouding her mind, as she entered the house. Her mum was with her aunts and uncles as well as brothers and their wives. She looked at her brothers who were very happy with their love lives, even her sister, she was glowing, as for her....life dealt her the wrong cards in the wrong game. She greeted them and headed for the kitchen. She bumped into Kenneth. Kenneth was one of the cute ushers at church. He always made small chit-chats with Abigail on numerous occasions at church, but she would just brush it off as friendliness from one church mate to another. "Sorry." "No, it was my fault." They both chuckled nervously. Then Abigail excused herself to the kitchen and grabbed a glass from the kitchen unit then poured herself a drink. She had a huge gulp before passing everyone in the sitting room and retiring to the bedroom. "Hey....your mum said I would find you in here." "Hi...again." Abigail forced a smile. He sat down next to her. "Are you ok?" He asked as he stared at her. "Yeah....I just have a little headache and with this new job taking all of my time, I barely have enough time to myself...anyway how about you?" He smiled. Trying to flirt. To get the message across. The message he has been throwing her way for a long time. They sat there as they started sharing stories about themselves with one another. Sharing laughs in between.

They went on for months. Hanging out whenever they had a chance and the more time they spent together the more Kenneth fell for her but the more she felt like she was not just deceiving him but herself as well. All that she could think about was not "embarrassing" her mother.

As Kenneth knelt down on one knee in front of the whole congregation, asking for her hand in marriage, she let tears rolled down her eyes. People thought they were tears of joy but only her sister, herself and God knew they were not. She was crying for herself. For her future. She let out a hard yes. Looking at her mother who was not just happy but ecstatic. She loved Kenneth like her own son.

When they got home she quickly went straight to the bedroom, that she once shared with her sister. Boingotlo followed her. "Why did you do that A?" "Do what? I'm getting married shouldn't you be happy?" "You are getting married to the wrong person Abby. You and I both know who you really are. You need to own it and live it…" She had this concern and sadness look. "You are making a ruckus." Mrs Mogale budged in. "What's all this noise about…." Boingotlo stared at Abigail as she folded her arms in front of her chest. Abigail shook her head tearing up as she mouthed "Please don't…" "Abigail shouldn't be getting married to someone she doesn't love." Boingotlo blurted out. A tear fell from Abigail's eye. "What are you talking about Boingotlo… is there someone that Abigail has feelings for?" "Yes….and it's not a he." Their mother froze. She felt a chill in mid-November. She turned to face Abigail who was in tears. "What is Boingotlo talking about?" Abigail trembled. She was shaking that she couldn't keep steady. "I'm les…." Before she could finish, her mother landed a very hot slap across her face.

"I will not hear any of this…is that understood Abigail? No daughter of mine will practice evil acts, understood." "But mum….." Her mother clenched her teeth together. "If you utter that word again I'm going to throw you out of this house." "Ever since I was young… I've been wondering why I haven't had any feelings for boys. Why I've never been in any relationship…all this time I thought it was because I was too busy to mingle but it was because, I was differently unique…." "There is nothing unique about going against the Bible." Her mother spat the words. "I fell head over heels for this amazing woman who had already accepted who she was and she made me realise the real me, I will not apologize for my sexuality mum…I am who I am and I can't change that." "What you say you are young lady is an abomination and I will not listen to any of this nonsense, because you are engaged to be married in April next year. You are going to marry Kenneth and you are going to love him and you are going to build a family do you understand me." "This is not some cold that I can just cough out or sleep off mother…." She slapped her again. "Come back to your senses right now Abigail." "But mum you can't force Abigail to be something that she is not…." She turned to face Boingotlo. "So you are the one who filled her with all of these crazy ideas. God does not approve of her stupidity and I will not allow my own daughter to condemn herself." "And who are you to judge someone? Huh, mother? "He who is without sin let him cast the first stone". Their mother froze. Abigail was hurt and confused at the same time. Boingotlo just stood her ground and looked at her mother in the eye. She didn't flinch.

As Abigail walked down the aisle, she clung onto every word that her mother said, when she tried to open up to her. She tried not to cry. She became numb even her feet moved with force as she tried to gracefully walk towards the man she doesn't even love, let alone see as a companion. Yes, Kenneth was the "perfect" guy. He was from a great family that brought him up well. He had his own company and he was rooted in the house of God, as well as grounded with God.

As they exchanged their vows Abigail's tears fell heavily. They exchanged rings and Boingotlo felt like her heart, could just burst as she watched her sister give up her true self to fit in the stereotype of what people call "normal". As the bride and groom were headed outside with people ululating and rejoicing she stood up and looked her in the eye, "I hope that your sacrifices are worth you losing yourself." She then left. She was not angry at her sister. No. She was sad and disappointed. Confused and paining. But mostly she didn't know how to feel about her mother. She knew how to play Abigail's feelings and she fell hard only getting herself hurt.

Daddy's Little Girl

Kgotso woke up to her own screaming. Her mum & stepdad came budging in. She was soaked wet from her sweating & tears had already dried up. "Do you still have them?" Her mum asked after switching on, the light and sitting down next to her. Kgotso nodded all out of breath. She stood up in her vest and panties. Took them off right in front of her parents & put on dry ones. "I'm sorry aI woke you guys." For some reason, there was a bit of guilt in her voice. Her stepdad hugged her. He felt her breasts against his pelvis. He almost lost control of his breath. His hands hung on tight to her. "It's ok…we know you are having a hard time forgetting what happened to you & your mum." She thought about what his father put her through. What she is holding back from her parents. Even still she found the strength to try to trust another man again. She hugged him back with all the embrace she had. She felt somewhat comfortable in his arms and his voice soothed her pain. They let go of each other, as she took a blanket from the closet and went to sleep in the sitting room with the tv on.

Kgotso was a very quiet & very well reserved young girl. She lived with her mother who was a nurse & stepfather, who was self-employed. He ran his business from home. She adored her parents but mostly her stepfather. He was overprotective of her. When Kgotso started senior school, she knew that she had a few years left until she leaves her parent's home and starts her own life, being the only child made it very hard for her to think about life without her parents.

Her mother came out of a very abusive relationship before she married Kabo, her stepfather. It was the same nightmare that kept her awake every night but the nightmare was more than she can chew. She was 6 years when she almost lost her mother as well as life. Her father was an abusive drunk who did nothing that could describe him as a father figure. She remembers waking up to hearing her mother screaming her lungs out. All house doors locked. Her father bellowing & howling, as well as cursing at the top of his lungs.

She dragged her feet to the passage to listen to her mother who was powerless over a man, who knew nothing about being a family protector. She curled into a ball. Her father found her crying and at that moment, he looked disgusted at her. "Why are you crying? For your slutty mum? Huh? Well I guess you are going, to grow up and be like her because an apple never falls too far from the tree." He then kicked her. She hit her head against the wall and all things faded into the background, even her own scream. Her own nightmare. She remembers yelling "I won't tell mum please stop….I won't tell anyone." The most painful part she wishes she can erase from her mind. She felt tainted and dirty.

Kgotso did not have friends at all. She was a lonesome. Even in junior school, she trusted the only two people in her life. As school started she told herself, that she was going to pass and make her parents proud. She had a vision board and everything. Her mum was proud of her and she loved her so much but she was concerned about her social life. So she encouraged her, to make at least one friend.

Kgotso was against the idea, but to put her mind at ease she thought about the one quiet girl who was always in her own little corner. She approached her and as time went by they became really close. They both had visions and it was something, that she never thought would happen to her.

As time went by, Kgotso spent most of her time with her stepdad and Onthatile since her mother worked night shifts at the clinic. Onthatile was a very beautiful young girl. Her skin tone was a little bit darker than Kgotso's, who was coffee-coloured. She had natural African hair. Her hourglass body made her even more irresistible to most guys at school. She and Kgotso visited one another, more often. They became instant sisters.

Kabo was fascinated by Onthatile and he always made sure, that he is home whenever she is around. There were times that Kgotso would catch him peaking through the bathroom door, whilst Onthatile was still bathing. But she paid no attention to it, because she thought he was just being protective or something. She trusted him.

One night Kgotso had her nightmare again. She woke up all soaked up by her sweat again, in the middle of the night. She sighed out loud as she dragged her feet to the kitchen, to have a glass of water. The chill that came from the water woke her up. She passed her parents room. It was closed and she heard some moanings and laughter. She just ignored. As she entered her room, she switched on her bedroom light. She almost choked on the water, as she took a sip. The other side of the bed was empty.

She felt a very cold chill running down her spine. She looked out the door to check if the bathroom or toilet light was still on. It was dark. She looked at the time, it was still early for her mum to be home. She shook off the feeling. She got undercovers and dozed off. The feeling that she had, made her numb to her wet sheets. She woke in the morning to find Onthatile next to her. She just kept quiet. As time went by, Kgotso became more irritated by having Onthatile at her place. She saw how all of a sudden she wore even more revealing clothes when she wanted to visit. She dolled up. She all of a sudden had money, to buy them lunch every single day. Kgotso started making excuses for having her at her place. She wanted to tell her mother the truth, but how can she do that when Kabo has been like a father to her. Always taking her shopping. Giving her enough money to do whatever she wants. She decided to confront Onthatile.

It was the final year of senior school and the third term was beginning. This means it has been almost a year since Onthatile and Kabo, have been having an affair. Kgotso was fed up with how Onthatile has changed. Kabo was also starting to become a little aggressive and distant. Her mum did not want to show it, but she was in a very bad space.

She entered the house and waited for Onthatile to take a sit. "Is my step-father the man you have been telling me about? The man who is always giving you money?? Please Onthatile, don't lie to me." Onthatile felt like oxygen failed her lungs. Her eyes started to flutter and glitter. Tears stung at the back of her eyeballs. She nodded as she couldn't make eye contact. Kgotso stood up, she looked even more disgusted. She didn't say a word but started to walk towards the door. As she reached for the door handle, "Please don't tell your mum, you know how much she adores me and loves Kabo. It will break her heart." Kgotso turned very fast and angrily, "Are you kidding me right now? Shouldn't you have thought about all of that, before you went on and opened those thighs of yours to my stepfather? You are crazy, right? You are the most selfish, the devil I have ever met in my life. It's true what they say, still waters run deep. All that quietness was just what, huh, pretence? You are something else you know that? You know what….?" Kgotso turned to leave. "Yes i'm selfish but do you know why I did it. I wanted to feel loved for once Kgotso. I wanted to feel wanted okay. Yes this body and these looks can get me any guy I want, but what about my needs being met? I was jealous okay that you had it all, a mum and dad that loves you. I wanted to play with Kabo, but I fell in too deep alright. He promised to take care of me as long as I keep, our friendship and also our affair a secret. He practically paid me to help him with his satisfaction and I admit, at one point it felt great to be treated like a woman, not a schoolgirl. I'm sorry for what happened. And besides, you should know better, by the way, he is always making googly eyes at you."

Kgotso stared at her blankly. "Oh come on. It's not that hard to see that Kabo lusts over you. You think he loves you like his own child? Chick open those Asian eyes of yours. The man wants to get into your panties." "Stop lying to make yourself look better, home-wrecking, slut." Onthatile's eyes widened. "Yeah and I slept with your dad so good, that he forgot his precious wife. What are you going to do about it, huh?" Kgotso couldn't believe what Onthatile said. She then banged the door behind her, without a word and left.

She got home with her head, still ringing Onthatile's words. She walked slowly past her parents' room, hoping that no one comes out. As she reached her bedroom door, she heard Kabo's voice behind her, "You were gone too long." "I went to see Onthatile. We had something to talk about." Kabo's facial expression changed. "What about?" She stared at him. "Nothing in particular just boys issues." "Oh!" He looked sternly at her. She then shrugged and headed inside her room.

She started to take off her jeans and top. As she was about to take off her bra, she had a very warm feature behind her. Hands started to caress her, from her hips to her cheek. She looked at the time. She made a curve at her lips. She turned and faced Kabo. His hands started to make a different movement. To her breasts, she gasped as he took them into his mouth. With that gasp, he knew she wanted him, as much as he did. "You wanna know a lil secret?" Kgotso said as she let out a moan. Kabo paused. He stood upright and looked at her in the eyes. She made a curve at her lips. She tiptoed as she flung her hands, around his neck. Feeling how hard he was in those boxers. "I'm not a virgin." She whispered. "Is that so?" Kabo said somewhat delighted. His hand found its way into her panty. She let out a loud moan, as he went deeper. "Yes…." She said as she landed a kiss on his mouth. "You wanna know who it was?" "Mmmhm" He said as he started to kiss her on the neck. "It was daddy." Kabo paused. Shocked. "I'm just telling you this, to let you know that I can keep a secret. I was daddy's little toy for a while. He told me not to tell anyone and I trust you…." She finished with another kiss, as she started kissing him going down. He sighed out loud. "I….can….keep….a…secret," she said slowly, while her hand was in his boxers.

He looked at her again, this time even more pleased. He picked her up, like the lightweight she is. He was wearing only his boxers. He slowly kissed her cheek. Her Forehead down her nose brushing against her mouth. He continued going down to her neck, then back to her breasts. Kgotso let out a little moan. His hands went to her panties and jerked them off. He then continued kissing her on her stomach, making her arch her back and continued going down as she arched her back with a moan. Her toes curling and tangling in those purple sheets. He went down on her for a few seconds, as she started to let out a very loud moan and gasp. Seeing that she was ready. He then took off his boxer and went in on her. Slowly. He was lost in her. He continued thrusting in and out. Slowly. He then started to move a little faster. With her legs wrapped around him. Her fingers dug into his back. Hanging on tight. She moaned so loud with passion.

He was way in too deep that he didn't hear, the front door opening and banging. She started to scream and kick at Kabo who was left in awe…Kgotso's mother felt numb at the sight of the scene. The last thing she wanted was to see her daughter hurt and it happened again. As the police dragged Kabo away, Kgotso curled next to her mother who was in so much….If only the same could be said about her.

From Beyond The Grave

It was not an ordinary Saturday morning, for the Ikhutseng family. Losing a loved one was never an easy feeling to get used to and burying them was the worst. Odirile lost more than a twin sister. He lost a best friend. Someone who was always there for him, especially since their parents are very strict and never gave them any attention. Now he doesn't know how he is going to continue living when a part of him has passed. As he watched the coffin going down, he almost jumped in after her.

When they got home he went straight to her bedroom. He went through her stuff, trying to find something and to his dismay, he found his sister's diary. For some reason, it was not locked. He thought twice before opening it. When he opened it a red square-shaped envelope fell out. He bent down and picked it up. It was addressed to him. He slowly opened it and inside, was a birthday card and a stack of letters. He opened the card and it was written, "Happy Birthday lil bro…. We might be twins but we both know who did the escape first….by the time you get this I will already be gone, so I wanted to give you one last gift before we really parted. Know that I love you so much and I know that, you will achieve both of our dreams for us. Hugs and kisses…"

He almost broke down in tears, as he fell on her bed. He forgot it was their 21st birthday and somehow, she knew he will get the card on that day. Even if she is gone she still knows him, better than anyone. He wanted to scream out loud, but he felt like there was something blocking his wind pipe. He tried to swallow but he couldn't. He then wiped the tears and unfolded the letters.

"Dear lil bro…

I know after you read this long letter you are going to be fuming with anger but please just let it go. Even though we are twins there were some secrets that i kept from you and i know you felt it because of our bond. Now that i'm gone i feel like i owe you an explaination of why i did what i did. I had no other choice because my life was now filled with a bunch of regrets, gulit trips, so much hate and pain. Remember that time when we were 8 years and dad wanted to take us to visit our uncle in Mochudi and you refused to go because you had to attend Kabelo's birthday party and i decided to just go because Kabelo is YOUR friend and not MINE, that's when my nightmare started. Uncle had a friend who always visited whenever we were there. No one paid attention to anything but he always brought me sweets and gave me money and i was a kid so i didn't mind. When uncle and dad left to go to the shops i told them that i was watching my favourite show so they can go without me.

The friend arrived. He asked me where dad and uncle went and i told him they just went out. That day i was wearing my favourite yellow dress. He sat down next to me and started touch me. From my ankles going up to my thighs. He smiled while doing it and kept saying i was beautiful and i'm already a woman. For some reason i felt something hurting deep inside of me. He took out a lollipop and said if i wanted it i should come and sit on his lap. I sat on him. And as i did that he lifted my dress and fixed me in a position that suited him. He gave me the lollipop and as i opened it i felt him touching me. He touched me and he just slid my panty to the side with his long huge fingers and i heard him entering me. He entered me and i felt something deep down breaking. It was not my heart but it could have been. He kept bouncing me up and down but it hurt. His hands held on tightly to my waist.

But it hurt. I couldn't scream or fight him beacuse we were alone….and it hurt even more. There was blood all over the couch, on him and on my beautiful dress.

When he was done he told me that he had fun playing with me and i shouldn't tell anyone about it. Not even my uncle because it would mean i would not be getting my sweets anymore. He then told me to go and bathe and tell them my period has started. I spent hours in the shower. Trying to wash him off. Trying to think why i let it happen. And like he said i lied to both dad and uncle. I was too paralyzed to even think of anything else. I know you remember when mum and dad wanted us to go visit uncle for some time but i refused. You saw something was wrong. I continued with that guilt for years. I started drinking and smoking when i was 15. That time when Thuto asked me to visit him at his place and I went even though you said i shouldn't, i wanted to feel that again. I guess i wanted to be sexed again because it built in. Kutlo was with Kabelo and Letso. I don't know what happened the only thing i remember drinking was a diet coke then i started to feel a little tipsy. Guess what? Yes they each took their turn and time, having their way with me. For some reason i enjoyed the moment even though i was too weak to move or do anything. When everything made sense the next day, that was when i decided i don't care about anything. If men can do that to me. If men can disrespect my body, who am i to try and respect myself. I felt worthless and cheap so I slept with a whole bunch of guys to try and numb the pain. I got addicted to sex so much i couldn't go a single day without it. When dad hit me that day when i came home drunk, it hurt, not because he beat me, no, it was because both mum and dad didn't even bother to ask me what was wrong. They just thought of my behaviour as a teenage rebel stage but that was not it. I was in pain and i know you felt that pain no matter how many times i pushed you away you continued to try and help me. You continued to be my brother, my best friend. Taking my life was the only way i could do damage control. With the different guys i slept with they each came with their own demons and diseases which i carried to the grave. I had more abortions than i could count. The last abortion that hospitalized me, mum and dad ignored me afterwards. I know you remember how things have been between me and our parents. They are not just mad at me, Odi. And it hurts for our parents to be like that towards us. Especially ever since the campaign started, they don't want any bad publicity that could hurt dad's chances of being MP. I did this to stop embarrassing mum and dad and also stop paining you because it ate at you as much as it did at me. I decided to be selfish for once. I know we had plans to have own brand and also go into the hospitality industry but i know you will fulfil those dreams for us.

Tell mum and dad that it pains me to see how strick they are without even trying to sit down and talk to us about our problems. Even if i had told them about my situation they wouldn't believe me because they have their head stuck so far into their lives that they forgot about us. I love you lil bro and i will always do even from beyond the grave.

Your already gone and forever loving sis?

:* : "

Odirile could not believe it. The whole room started to spin. The walls started to close in on him. The roof caved in on him. He started to suffocate. Oxygen failed his lungs. He was not asthmatic nor did have any illness, but for some reason he felt like he was having both asthma and heart attack. His chest was burning. His throat dried out. His head was not just aching, but it felt like someone hit him so hard against the wall. He passed out with the letters falling out of his hand. When he opened his eyes he saw his parents and some of his family members in the room. They moved him to his own room. His father was angry. "Are you trying to go after your sister?" Odirile just stared at his father.

"Odirile we know today has been a rough day for you but it has been for us too, ok….we know how you feel." At that moment Odirile lost it. He stood up in front of his parents and stared at them blankly. The family members excused themselves when his father cleared his throat. " Odirile we know…." His mother moved closer to him, he was fuming. He brought his eyebrows together and… "How could you possibly know how I feel when you don't know a single thing about me? When you didn't know what was happening with Oagile? Tell me that mum!" He shouted at the top of his voice.

His father was so angry that he struck him. He did not care whether he just woke up or not. He will not be disrespected. "You will not bring this foolishness into my house and you watch your tone when talking to us…we are your parents, not peers." A tear fell from his eye, "That's all you know, taking action without listening first. I don't mean to be disrespectful to both of you, but you two are the lousiest parents ever. I lost my sister because you two were too busy, thinking about your fake pretence parental guidance when you lacked it yourself. Oagile committed suicide so stop telling people, that it was an accident of some sort. She was raped at the age of 8…..8 years old." His mother lost balance. His father stayed speechless. "She was going through a lot but because you are too old to understand the pain of your children, she took her life because life dealt hard with her. If you don't believe me…." He stood up and went to her room. He found the letters on the floor and took them. He sighed out loud as he returned to his parents and threw the letters on the bed. "….read those and maybe you will get a clear view, if not a glimpse of the kind of pain that your daughter went through. I know you won't feel it like I do, but I hope the guilt stays and entraps you." He then turned to leave.

He then saw Kabelo walking towards him, from the leaving room. Before he could say a word, he landed a very huge blow to his face. He lost his balance and fell to the floor, "That was for my sister you spineless jerk. Now get the hell out of my house before I drag you out." Kabelo seemed somewhat surprised. "I know you raped my sister and you better say your prayers, because once my parents finish reading the letter that she left of you and your buddies drugging and gang-raping her….buddy I don't wanna be here right now if I was you. Now leave." He then walked over him and left the house. He walked out without hesitating or looking back.

...My Heart Didn't

Growing up I always admired my parents. They always had this great bond, that you would think it's a teenage dream. Yes they had their fair share of fights, but they resolved their issues with so much maturity. I have to admit I loved that. I have been in a relationship with this amazing guy, who we have so much in common and one could swear that we were related. I told him about my parents, and how I want to have something a little similar to what they have. He told me about his father who has been the only parent he knew because his mum passed away when he was three years.

We could talk for hours without getting bored and I know some people, would not believe me when I told them this but we haven't done anything yet. We just made out a lot but we never went further than that. With me being in tertiary and finally in my final year and him always working hard to get the promotion at the law firm he was working for, we never really had time to spend so much time together or even talk about family and anything. It has been like that for the past three years, but we didn't mind because we know what we want in life and I loved that about him. He was grounded and had a good head on his shoulders. We just lived in the moment and we loved it, that way because it meant we never had to worry about trust issues or communication issues or any other issues. Mum and I were so close and we shared basically everything, from my love life to her advice and guess she is the reason I still have stability in my life. Dad is a bit strict but he is a man after all right. Having a lil brother is great, until he annoys the living daylights out of you.

One could say we are a perfect family, but we are just an ordinary Botswana family. Mum hasn't seen Pako or talked to him or anything, but she nags me from time to time about meeting him and I told her it wasn't time yet. "Are you still refusing to give me anything about Pako?" Mum said as she sat next to me in the living room. I looked at her and shrugged. I lived alone. I wanted to learn to be independent and they fully supported it, even though dad was a little sceptical about it eventually he caved. I visited them whenever I was free.

"You know I love you mum, but Pako is not the topic you wanna argue with me about." I looked at her and gave her a very laid back smile. Dad and Tlotso walked in. They were from the Saturday soccer game. Even though Tlotso was six years he enjoyed it more, especially since he spent time with dad. "Can you at least give me a last name or something?" She flattered her long fake eyelashes. I smiled and stood up preparing to leave. "Hi dad, bye dad and may you please tell my mum to wipe her nose because she has a little bit of my business on it." Dad laughed as he hugged me. "I told you, babe, she won't cave and technically I don't wanna know the guy who has been keeping you away from us because you barely visit." He said, as I rubbed Tlotso's head and gave him a light kiss. "I know dad that you are dying to meet him and…kill him." "You read my mind." He said as he walked towards mum, bending over her to give her a light kiss.

I smiled and shook my head, as I stood by the door. "I love you guys but you know, the reason I moved is because of…..that," I said when I pointed at them when they kissed. Tlotso chuckled as he ran to his room. They just laughed and dad went to their bedroom. "Can you at least promise me that you will be careful out there?" "You know I always am…." I looked at my phone that was ringing and smiled as I said "You know I always am mum…now I have to go. I'm meeting Pako. He said he wanted us to eat out tonight….byeeeee." I closed the door behind me and answered the phone.

We met at both our favourite restaurant. I know it's crazy but yes we have our very own favourite place, even though we are complete strangers and funny enough it's where we met the first time 3 years ago. He stood up and gave me a huge hug and landed a kiss on my mouth.

"Hey, babe." He said as we sat down. "So is your mum still nosy about my identity?" I looked at him over the menu with a raised eyebrow. He threw in a hysterical laughter. "I'm glad you find this amusing." I sat the menu down. The waitress came and we ordered. As she left I looked at him. He had this huge smile plastered on his face, the same smile he had when he graduated but this one was much bigger. It went from one ear to the other.

"So I have some good news and amazingly great news....which one do you want to hear first?" He said as he held my hands in his. I looked at him, mirror imaging his smile. "Let's start with the good news." I said curiously. "I got the promotion...." Now my smile got even wider. "Really babe?" I squealed and squeezed his hands even tighter. He nodded with that huge smile still plastered. "Ok this is worth celebrating my love....this is huge....now for the great news."

"Katlego you know I love you right." "I do babe....& I do too... so much." "And ever since I was up for this promotion I have been thinking about one thing and that is a future with the future Mrs me." He reached into the pocket of his jacked. My heart skipped several beats. "I know you don't do engagements and you are not a huge fan of it....but..." "Babe....don't..." I tried to argue with him but he took out the ring from the box. It was not an expensive ring with a huge diamond on it. It was just simple with a silver and a small diamond on top. He knew I didn't do engagements but he still went on anyway. "This is not a booking my love....this is not a promise... this is me saying I want you to stay and let us be a part of each other's lives forever. We've been through a lot together. I cheated on you a couple of times but you stayed. We are not perfect but I'll rather be imperfect with you than be out there searching. I'm in love with you Miss Atlegang...." And with the last statement, he had me hooked. He liked to tease me with my surname and he knew it was my weakness. I smiled and I agreed. I was not happy... I was ecstatic. Over the moon. He stood up and he picked me up and gave me a huge hug. He was a little bit taller than me. I felt his bass drum beating heart.

We went back to his place and one thing led to another. He was my first and it was the best night of my life. Two months passed and we were still very much in love and had just written my final paper. We had decided to tell my mum about everything and allow him to meet my family finally. My mum was seated down when I entered and Pako followed me. Dad was still in the kitchen. Mum stared at us. For some reason she looked like she has seen a ghost. "Mum." She came back to earth with her phone still in her hands. "Yes hon." She faked a smile. I knew that smile because it was the smile I always gave out when I met people I didn't like.

"You must be Pako." "Yes ma'am." They shook hands and we sat down next to each other. "Kat is that you?" Dad shouted from the kitchen. "Yes dad, and I finally kept mum quiet." He came out holding a glass of juice. He cleared his throat. Pako stood up and shook dad's hand. He had mum's look. "So this is the Pako I've been telling you about." "What is your last name Pako." "Motlotlegi." We both said. "And where are you from?" Pako cleared his throat and "Well my dad said he moved to Palapye after my mum passed when I was three but I was born here in Serowe and I decided to move back here after I graduated from BIUST!" Mum's eyes glittered. "And I wanted to share the good news with you guys…..he asked me to marry him." Mum gasped.

She covered her mouth and stood up to leave. Dad followed her. I looked at Pako. "Maybe we came at a bad time." He said. "Yeah…. maybe." I looked more confused than him. I stood and prepared some snacks for the both of us. We waited as we chatted and laughed for some minutes. "I'm sorry about that guys…it was just a long day." Mum came back with red swollen eyes. I tried to ignore but it was hard not to because we had an awkward lunch with mum still giving fake smiles and laughs in between conversations. Tlotso was at uncle Rebaone's place, visiting his cousins for the weekend.

When it was time to leave, we decided that Pako leave and I stay to speak to my parents. We stayed silently for a while with mum and dad giving each other looks. "If you guys didn't like Pako you can just say it…please because the minute we walked in you guys have been faking everything.

The convos…the laughs…the smiles…." They whispered to each other. "Seriously? I'm here…I asked you the question parents…." "Can you ask Pako to come back tomorrow?" I gave out a light scoff, "After the way you treated him today….I don't think that's a great idea." Mum stood up and sat next to me, her eyes even more swollen. She held my hands in hers. She was shaking. "Please baby Kat…it's very important. Please!" I was scared. I didn't know what to do or say. I stared at dad who looked blank and away from us."Ok." I agreed.

"Do you think this is a great idea?" I asked him as we got out of the car and he came around and had me against the car. His right hand at my waist and with the left one he supported himself. I felt his warmth and heartbeat. Our hearts were in perfect sync. He gave me the car keys to keep in my bag. "Babe I want to spend the rest of my life with you and I need your parents to be on our side…I need my in-laws and besides not having a mum sucks. It's been me and dad against the world even though he isn't the perfect father but still….I love having a woman around and I want our kids to have something I never had….I want a huge family with both parents." I smiled and gave him a huge kiss on his lips. We walked in and as we did Pako froze at the door.

"Dad?" I looked puzzled. "What are you doing here?" Pako asked as we sat down. "Mum…what's going on?" Everyone in the house looked at one another. The tension and awkwardness were so thick that you could cut it with a knife. Mum started to open her mouth. My mind started to spin out of control. My blood pressure shot up… so high that I felt the whole room spinning. I stood up and looked at everyone. I made a hysterical laugh. "You are joking right? I mean this is just another one of your jokes right mum…mum…" She shook her head with tears flooding down her cheeks. "Dad….dad?" I turned to the man I grew up calling "dad". He also didn't look at me.

"Pako can't be my brother. He just can't. We are to get married. Start a family.....why on earth would you lie like that?!" "I'm afraid. Your parents are not lying to you. When I walked out on your mum with Pako, we both didn't know that she was pregnant…with you but she told me later and we decided that I keep Pako because she couldn't manage to take care of two kids let alone one." Pako's dad stared at us. Pako was silent. In shock. He was shaking. "What kind of parents, split up siblings! What kind of grudge did you guys have for each other, that you would punish us…huh?! Do you know how torn I am right now….you told me that my mother was dead. You said she was freaking dead?" I've never seen Pako that angry. He was shaking. His jawline was more visible than before. Tears rolled down his eyes. He shouted at his father but the truth hit me harder than his anger. I looked at mum who was in tears. She kept apologising over and over and over again. I felt nauseous and quickly ran to the toilet. Everything I ate just came out but mum's words still rung so loud in my ears and mind. My heart did not break…it got smashed into a million pieces.

I went back to the living room and Pako quickly rushed beside me and held on to me. "Are you ok?" "Yeah…I'm just feeling a little light-headed." He sat me down and at that moment I couldn't look at him the same. "Katlego are you pregnant?" Mum said as she stared at me. "Yes mum I am….I was going to….." I paused. The realisation hit me…hard! I Cried. I wanted to scream. I felt a huge blockage in my throat but it was too huge to swallow. I looked at both of my "fake parents" and "I hate you!" I then left. Mum tried to stop me but I just took the car and left.

I remember waking up in the hospital with plasters and bandages on my head and arm. I fell unconscious while still driving and ran through a green traffic light. The truck couldn't stop in time. It hit the car on my side and swayed out the road. According to the doctor, I had a dislocated shoulder. Bruised head and some bruises almost all over the body and lastly I lost my child. The child that I share with my brother. I committed incest with my own brother. Not half or step but 100% biological brother. It hurt because he was my first. It hurt because I believed he was my future. It hurt because our parents lied to us. The man I thought was my father, turned out to be my stepfather. My whole life was a lie.

I couldn't even look at my parents the same way. I couldn't look at Pako the same way. As they all entered the room I looked away and "Please leave....all of you!"

Ever since then I never wanted to be in a relationship. I never looked at any guy the same way. As I looked at the ring Pako gave me for the last time before putting it in an envelope with a letter, my heart sunk. His job transferred him to their other branch in Namibia, it came with the promotion. He has been trying to reach out to me, as well as my parents but I couldn't face any of them so I just decided to go into hibernation and flight mode.

It has been a year since I entered that house after my whole world went under. I looked at the three of them. For some reason I felt nothing looking at them. I no longer felt anger towards them. I was angry for so long, that I couldn't anymore. I walked towards them and stood. "I'll say what I have to say and leave, because I have to go finish packing..." "Packing?" Mum whispered under her breath. I looked at her. She looked like she hasn't slept in months. So many eye bags under her eyes. She even had a bare face. No long fake eyelashes or any sort of make up.

"Whatever went down between you and....him..." I pointed at my... "father". It was hard to swallow the lie that turned to be a painful fact, let alone say the word. "...was petty and cruel to us and also it was a selfish move. I always wondered why Pako and I, had so much in common it was because we were..." I couldn't finish. I took a deep breath and continued. "I came here to say I'm sorry...for the pain and ignorance for the past year but I just needed time out.... from you and the whole world and know that I'm not mad at you. I'm actually done being mad. I can't hate my parents because God will not forgive me. I just wanted to say goodbye to you guys and give this to

Tlotso. I know you lied to him as well about my whereabouts but then again that's what you guys are good at, right. I'm going to further my studies in Malaysia and I wanted to say my farewell to the three of you. I don't hold grudges, even though you lied to me my whole life there are some great things you taught me which I'm proud to value so for that thank you."

Before mum could say anything I turned to leave. "Please don't… I've already made up my mind and I'm trying to avoid saying things, that I will regret my whole life." She sniffed and "I love you baby and thank you as well for making me a proud mother as well as a parent. I hope you prosper and let your light shine brighter than the morning star. Mostly thank you for your forgiveness." Something in my heart became alive and I made a smile, at the corner of my lips then left.

White Flag

I stood in front of the crowd in my royal blue dress, with my husband by my side. Friends and family cheering and applauding. I forced a huge grin trying to hide the pain I felt at that moment. We were celebrating our 10 years anniversary. Yes we have been married for more than 10 years. Such a milestone I know but at that moment it felt like a knife to the heart. I had a huge gulp stuck at my throat. No matter how many times I tried to swallow or wash it down with a drink, there was no change at all. He pulled me closer to him by the waist and I clenched my fist, so tight that my nails dug through my palm and leaving a bloody trailed mark of nails. He looked at me and I couldn't bring myself to giving him even a stare.

As people came from every part of the garden to congratulate us, I let a couple of tears hit the grass. I excused myself to the restroom to get fixed. I looked in the mirror and for some reason I saw a different person. A weak, pathetic loser that I never thought I would become. Let me take you to the genesis of our lives. As to why I feel pain and not joy, on my 10th anniversary. I have always been the type of girl that was committed and had so much respect for every person in my life, which helped paved the way to my success. My husband has been the best kind of husband anyone can ever wish for. He has taken care of me and my family ever since we started dating. You see I'm from a very poor background. I am the youngest child and I didn't do well at school. I failed my form five and life dealt roughly with me. My two brothers were both addicts, one to alcohol and the other to smoking anything that he could. It was up to me to see to it that, I try to atleast help my parents. It hurt because I was the last born, yet I had to toughen up and act like the eldest child. I found a job at Saverite. Even though Kumakwane was a small like really small village, it had its bright side-ish. My salary was not enough to sustain the whole family, but it filled a couple of holes. My mum and dad were receiving their elderly payments and still, I was responsible for going with them to the post office to collect. At times I would cry myself to sleep thinking, about the heavy burden I carried on my shoulders.

Kabelo became my saviour when I least expected it. I was walking home late at night and three guys had been waiting outside when I knocked off. They followed me very quietly and as further, I went the darker the path became. The hair at the back of my neck stood up. I got a very cold chill in the middle of September. I walked a bit faster with my arms folded in front of my broad chest. As one was about to grab my shoulder, a car came from behind and brightened its front headlights. The drunk slender man let go. As the car approached, I moved a bit slowly with my head on the ground and fright filled, my bass drum beating heart. The car parked beside me. The windows were tinted. The windows slowly rolled down and a deep voice, from the car said, "Babe, why didn't you wait for me?" For some reason, I felt relieved. I reached for the door handle and one of the men tried to block me. He smelt of a horrible mixture of alcohol and smoke. His messy uncombed hair made him look like he has not had a bath in weeks. I heard the door from the driver's side opening. I don't know how or when, but he was by my side, with just one step or maybe it was two. I couldn't see properly because my mind, was on my hand that was held so tightly by the other man.

With just one blow, the guy fell to the ground and he lost his grip on my hand. He looked at the other men so fiercely, and boldly said, "Unless you want a piece of what he just had, I suggest you move." They moved aside and he opened the door with his other hand as the other one was over my shoulders. I got in then he closed the door. His car was so clean and smelt so fresh like him. His musk body spray was all over me. I could feel it from just that over the shoulders touch. He dropped me off at my place. To my surprise, he knew where I lived. He didn't even ask for directions. He got out and opened the door again. He went on and opened the gate. He still had his hand over my shoulders and I couldn't help, but lean in to him. I was still mesmerised by his gesture and his cologne. He came in greeted my parents and told them everything.

For some reason he didn't mind, sitting by the fire and having simple pap and meat. He seemed to enjoy it. My parents were not those types of strict parents. They were open with me about everything and I was to them as well. Our relationship was one of the things I cherished. Even though we were not well off. We were rich at heart. As I walked him back to his car, I wanted to ask as to how did he know, "Boago Keotlhopile, form 5S. The most quiet girl I have ever met. You take the same route to work every day and when you come back you use the gravel road which you believe is much safer. You always wear your shirt with dark blue jeans or black trousers. During lunch, you sit by a certain corner, alone and eat whatever you have and sometimes you don't eat but still you have the energy to work and put a smile on your face everyday. You always make sure you carry atleast a plastic of bread or meat back home everyday. I admire you Boago. Your brothers should be the ones working their asses off, for the family but instead they are wasting their lives at that shebeen everyday. You are a strong young woman and families need more daughters like you. Anyway thank you for such an amazing night." I was smitten. He kissed my forehead and said, "Take care." Just like that he disappeared into the dark.

Days turned into months with Kabelo, picking me up from work everyday. Did I mention? Kabelo was my former schoolmate at Naledi Senior School. It turns out he liked me back then, but he never had the courage to approach me. Apparently he thought I was "way above his league". I laughed when he told me that. He had passed his form five and at the age of 21, he had already started his own business. Kabelo was an orphan. He was raised by his uncle and aunt. Their mistreatments did not let him give up instead, they built him. He gave my brothers jobs. To my surprise he was able to keep them, on the straight and narrow.

He built my parents a new house, connected water and electricity. We became the whispers of the town. Rumours to be exact. We were called witches. People said we have bewitched him. He did not care. He was the most care-free human I have ever met. He would just brush it off and say, "Let rumours just be rumours babe. We both know the truth and that's what matters." He helped pay for me to further my studies. I got a better paying job at some company. I told him I wanted to earn my way. A few months later, he sent his uncles for the lobola negotiations. I had no idea that he was even considering to marry me. A simple rural girl who didn't care about the new trending fashion or any make up. Within a few weeks, we were already married because he said he couldn't wait, to spend the rest of his life with me.

Years passed and we were still happy. We had our own house and our two bundles of joy. The amount of blessing that I had, was more than enough. I felt like God was making up for the times, that He allowed suffering to toy with me.

I have no idea what came over me that day. The day I decided to repay my hero's kindness, with betrayal and pain and secrets. His name was Onkabetse. He was one of Kabelo's business dealings associates. The man had broad shoulders. Cute dimples and everytime he smiled, I became weak at my knees. With just one touch and kiss, I gave in to temptation to my satisfaction. He would make random visits to our house unanounced and that would please me. I started to change the way I dressed. I dressed more sexier. Tight skirts or pants.

I wore make up. I had my nails done almost every two weeks, as for my hair. I made sure I was up to date. My husband noticed and he didn't say anything. My whole wardrobe and image changed, because of one man. A man who doesn't know my heart but my body. He gave me pleasure in so may ways. I started to glow. My husband still kept quiet and became the amazing and caring man I met almost 10 years ago.

A month was left for us to celebrate, our 10th anniversary. He had planned for us to renew our vows. I remember seeing the pain in his eyes, when he walked in on us on our matrimonial bed. He was supposed to go for a business trip to Kasane, but it got cancelled so he thought he would surprise his "loving wife". I had already sent the kids to my parent's house. He still didn't say anything when he walked in on us. He just looked at us and went out. I asked Onkabetse to leave quickly and he did.

That night my husband for the very first time came home drunk. He found me in the living room and sat next to me. "How did I fail you Boago? I mean I gave you everything any woman could ever wish for. I gave you my heart and you just tossed it away. I gave you my time and life. You toyed with them. Please tell me…" He turned to look at me with tears filled in his eyes. "How did I fail you? Maybe I can try to fix it." At the sight of my husband's agony, I felt my heart leaping out of its place and blocking my wind pipe. "You are the perfect man. The perfect father. With him it was just about sex….I'm sorry…I just don't know what came over me. I just lost sight of us…" "It was just sex? Why didn't you tell me that I was doing something wrong? I could have changed. I could have made love to you better. I could have watched those romantic movies or read those sex books so that I could satisfy you…why didn't you talk to me. I love you Kutlwano's mum, you know I would die for you… I just…I just need to sleep." I held on to him from behind whipping and screaming and stuttering. Asking for forgiveness. He just became cold. The phase that he has never showed me. I slept on the sofa that night.

He had woken up early in the morning and made breakfast. He woke me up with a forehead kiss. "Go and take a bath babe." He said sweetly. He smelled so sweet in the morning. His cologne has not changed. It took me back to the day that we met. I was surprised. I expected him to be cold like last night but no, he was the Kabelo I fell for. I took a long bath trying to wash my guilt off but I couldn't. As I got out he offered me breakfast. We sat down in the living room and watched tv. He smiled at me and said. You look beautiful queen B. That was his pet name for me. I made a weak smile and said ""Thank you." "Now have your breakfast before it gets cold." I ate cautiously. He realised then took a forkful from my plate and ate with a smile.

As the day progressed, we had to go and collect the kids from my parent's. We went in the same car. He was his happy self and that scared me. We got there and everyone was happy. He took out the plastic bags from the boot and gave some to me as he smiled at me when our kids came laughing, running and jumping towards us. I hugged them so tight and embraced every moment. We spent a few hours with the family before heading back.

We got home late that day and I just prepared the kids for bed. I sat by the dining table with my thoughts running around. He came and faced me, "Next month we are celebrating our 10th anniversary. So here is how it's going to play out. We are going to continue to be the happy couple that we are, and you are going to continue to be a loving and loyal wife until death do us apart and when I mean death, I mean natural death. If you try to kill yourself, I'm going to stop supporting your parents and take back my house. As for your brothers, let's just say they will go to jail and they will never see the light of day as long as I am alive. This here is a document that you are going to sign. It's my last will and testament. I am leaving everything to my children. When I die they can throw you out, whenever they want. If you try to leave me, I am going to file for full custody and you are going to go back to poverty. You are my wife and that is how it will remain…" With tears rolling down my cheeks I asked, "Why would you do this to me?" He simply said, "Because I made you and I can break you. But mostly you, my dear, loving wife, triggered the beast. The most cruel and devious beast. Now be a good wife and let's go make love…" He grinned as he picked me up and took me to our bed. As he kissed my cheeks and then my lips, I gave in because I was responsible for what he has become. He said he made me, now I fear I created an opposite version of him.